Pen

ANNE OF
GREEN GABLES

L. M. MONTGOMERY

LEVEL

2

RETOLD BY HANNAH DOLAN
ILLUSTRATED BY RENIA METALLINOU
SERIES EDITOR: SORREL PITTS

PENGUIN BOOKS

UK | USA | Canada | Ireland | Australia
India | New Zealand | South Africa

Penguin Books is part of the Penguin Random House group of companies
whose addresses can be found at global.penguinrandomhouse.com.
www.penguin.co.uk www.puffin.co.uk www.ladybird.co.uk

Penguin
Random House
UK

Penguin Readers edition of *Anne of Green Gables* published by Penguin Books Ltd, 2021

002

Original text written by L. M. Montgomery
Text for Penguin Readers edition adapted by Hannah Dolan
Text for Penguin Readers edition copyright © Penguin Books Ltd, 2021
Illustrated by Renia Metallinou
Illustrations copyright © Penguin Books Ltd, 2021
Cover illustration by Chris Silas Neal

Printed and bound in Great Britain by Clays Ltd, Elcograf S.p.A.

The authorized representative in the EEA is Penguin Random House Ireland,
Morrison Chambers, 32 Nassau Street, Dublin D02 YH68

A CIP catalogue record for this book is available from the British Library

ISBN: 978-0-241-49308-3

All correspondence to:
Penguin Books
Penguin Random House Children's Books
One Embassy Gardens, 8 Viaduct Gardens,
London SW11 7BW

Contents

People in the story

Mrs. Rachel Lynde

Matthew Cuthbert

Marilla Cuthbert

Anne Shirley

Diana Barry

Gilbert Blythe

New words

carrots

medicine

puffed sleeves

raspberry juice

wine

woods

Note about the story

At a young age, Lucy Maud Montgomery (1874–1942) lived on Prince Edward Island—a very small part of easten Canada. In 1905, she wrote her first and most famous book, *Anne of Green Gables*.

The book tells the story of Anne, an eleven-year-old **orphan*** from Nova Scotia—a bigger part of easten Canada. Anne goes to live with Matthew and Marilla Cuthbert on their farm, Green Gables, on Prince Edward Island. She is a happy and intelligent girl. But she sometimes talks too much, and she often makes **mistakes**!

Lucy Maud Montgomery wrote lots more books about Anne. *Anne of Green Gables* was also a film and on TV.

Before-reading questions

1 Look at the cover of the book. Think about these questions:
   a What kind of person is Anne, do you think? How do you know this?
   b What is Green Gables? Where is it, do you think?
   c What will the story be about, do you think?
2 The story starts in the 1880s. What do you know about Canada at that time?
3 What things were different for boys and girls at that time?
4 Look at the "People in the story" on page 4. Choose one of the people (not Anne), and write about them.

*Definitions of words in **bold** can be found in the glossary on pages 63–64.

CHAPTER ONE
Something strange

It was 3.30 p.m. on a sunny June day in Avonlea. Mrs. Rachel Lynde sat at her window. She watched everything and everyone in Avonlea. Strange things did not often happen there, but Mrs. Lynde always watched for them anyway.

Suddenly, Matthew Cuthbert drove past on the road out of Avonlea. Now this *was* strange! Matthew Cuthbert did not leave his home very often. He was a quiet man. He did not like going anywhere different, and he did not like talking to new people.

"Why is Matthew driving out of town, and why is he wearing his best clothes?" said Mrs. Lynde. "I must know."

Mrs. Lynde could not rest. "I will go to Green Gables and ask Marilla. She will tell me," she thought.

Matthew and his sister, Marilla, lived at Green Gables—a house near the woods. It was away from the other houses in Avonlea. They liked that.

Mrs. Lynde walked to Green Gables. "Come in," she heard from behind the kitchen door.

Marilla Cuthbert sat at the kitchen table. There were three plates on it.

"Someone is coming here for dinner," Mrs. Lynde thought.

Marilla was a tall, thin woman with dark hair.

"Good evening, Rachel," said Marilla. "How are you?"

"I'm well, but how are you, Marilla?" asked Mrs. Lynde. "I was **worried**. I saw Matthew driving out of town."

"I'm fine," answered Marilla. "Matthew went to Bright River train station. An **orphan** boy is coming from an **orphanage** in Nova Scotia. He will help Matthew on the farm."

"Marilla! What are you thinking? You are bringing a strange child into your home. You know nothing about him," said Mrs. Lynde.

"That is true, Rachel. But we will know him soon," said Marilla.

Mrs. Lynde wanted to stay until Matthew came home, but she also wanted to tell people the news. She left quickly, and Marilla was happy. She did not want to talk to Mrs. Lynde about the orphan.

CHAPTER TWO

Matthew and Marilla are surprised

At Bright River, the train station was quiet. Matthew could only see a little girl.

"When will the five-thirty train be here?" he asked the man in the ticket office.

"The five-thirty train left. That little girl was on it. She is waiting for you," the man answered.

"But I came for a boy. I don't understand," said Matthew.

"You can ask her about it," the man said, quickly. He wanted to go home for his dinner.

Matthew was very frightened of new people. "What can I say to this little girl?" he thought.

The little girl watched Matthew. She was eleven years old. She wore an ugly yellow dress and a brown hat. Her face was small, white, and thin, and she had bright red hair.

"Are you Mr. Matthew Cuthbert of Green Gables?" she asked. "I am happy to see you! I thought about sleeping in a tree tonight, but going home with you is much better."

"I'm sorry I was so late," Matthew said, quietly. He could not tell the little girl about the **mistake**.

"I'll take her home," he thought. "Marilla will tell her."

The little girl talked a lot on the drive to Green Gables. "Prince Edward Island is very pretty. Look at that cherry tree over there with all the white flowers!" she said, happily. "Well, this is wonderful. I'm going to live with you and have a home. I always wanted a home."

Matthew enjoyed listening to this intelligent and funny girl. "We will make her very sad," he thought, "because she can't stay."

Later that evening, Matthew walked through the door of Green Gables with the little girl.

"Who is that? Where is the boy?" asked Marilla.

"There was no boy," said Matthew. "Only *her*." Matthew looked at the little girl in the yellow dress. He did not know her name.

The child's face was suddenly sad.

"You don't want me because I'm not a boy!" she said. "Nobody wants me." She started crying very hard.

Marilla was **surprised**. "Don't cry about it," she said.

The child looked up. "But I'm very sad! I thought I had a home, and now I don't. Because I'm not a boy!" she shouted.

Marilla smiled a little. "Please stop crying. You can stay tonight, and we can talk again in the morning. What's your name?"

"Will you please call me Cordelia?" said the child.

"Is that your name?" asked Marilla.

"Well, no. But I would like to be called Cordelia," she said.

"Cordelia is not your name. What is?" said Marilla.

"Anne Shirley," she said, sadly. "But I like Cordelia better."

"Anne is a good, **sensible** name," said Marilla.

"All right, but please call me Anne with an 'e.' It looks much nicer."

"Were there any boys at the orphanage?" Marilla asked Anne.

"Yes, there were lots of boys, but you wanted a girl, they said. Would you like a girl with brown hair better than me?" asked Anne.

"No, your hair doesn't matter. We need a boy to help Matthew on the farm," said Marilla.

———————

Anne could not eat anything at dinner.

"You are not eating," said Marilla.

"I can't. I **feel** too sad. Have you felt this sad before?" asked Anne.

"No," said Marilla.

"Then you do not understand. It feels **terrible**. You can't eat bread, cake, chocolate, or anything."

"Anne looks tired, Marilla," said Matthew, kindly.

Marilla took Anne to bed, then came back to the kitchen. "She must go back to the orphanage, Matthew," she said, quietly.

"But she's a nice little thing, Marilla," Matthew said. "Maybe she can stay, and I can find a boy to help me on the farm."

"No, Matthew. We don't need a girl, and she talks too much," said Marilla.

"OK," said Matthew. He went to bed. Then Marilla went to bed. Anne cried in her bed until she slept.

CHAPTER THREE
Anne's story

The next morning was bright and sunny. Anne saw a pink cherry tree from her bedroom window and felt happy. Then she remembered—she could not stay at Green Gables, because she was not a boy.

Anne looked out at the pretty garden and **daydreamed** for a long time.

Suddenly, Anne felt Marilla's hand on her. "Breakfast is ready now," Marilla said.

Anne stood up. "Green Gables is beautiful. I'm sad because I can't stay. But I will always remember it," she said, brightly.

"Put on your dress, and remember to wash your face," said Marilla.

Anne was at the kitchen table in ten minutes. She wanted to make Marilla happy.

"I'm hungry today," Anne said to Marilla and Matthew at the table. "Things don't feel as bad this morning. I like mornings. Do you like mornings? It's a nice, sunny morning, but I like rainy mornings, too."

"Please stop talking!" said Marilla. "You talk too much, Anne."

Anne did not speak again, and they all ate breakfast.

Marilla watched Anne closely. "It is strange to see her sitting quietly," she thought.

After breakfast, Marilla asked Anne a question. "Where did you live before the orphanage?"

"In Bolingbroke, Nova Scotia," said Anne. "My father's name was Walter Shirley, and my mother's name was Bertha Shirley. They were teachers. I don't remember our house, but I think about it a lot. In my **daydreams**, it's very pretty, with lots of flowers."

"My mother got **sick** and died. I was only three months old. Then my father died, and I was an orphan," Anne said.

Marilla listened quietly to Anne. "What happened after that?" she asked, softly.

"I lived with our cleaner, Mrs. Thomas, because my mother and father didn't have any family. She was very poor and had an angry husband. I helped with their children until I was eight. Then, Mr. Thomas died suddenly, and Mrs. Thomas didn't want me. Someone called Mrs. Hammond took me, and I helped with her eight children. It was hard work! I lived with Mrs. Hammond for two years, and then she moved away. I went to the orphanage after that, and now I'm here."

Anne did not like telling her story. It made her feel too sad. She liked talking about beautiful things in the world.

"Did you go to school?" asked Marilla.

"Only at the orphanage," Anne answered. "But I can read. I love reading books."

Marilla felt sorry for Anne. "Maybe Anne *can* stay," she thought. "She talks too much, but she is sweet and intelligent."

———

Later that day, Marilla talked to Matthew. "You're right about Anne—she can live with us. I don't know much about children, and I will make mistakes. But I will teach her things," she said.

Matthew smiled. "I'm very happy about this, Marilla."

"I'll tell her tomorrow," said Marilla.

CHAPTER FOUR
Mrs. Lynde

The next day, Marilla asked Anne to wash the dishes and clean the floors. "She is a hard worker," Marilla thought. "But sometimes she daydreams too much and forgets about her work."

Anne felt worried. "Miss Cuthbert," she said, after dinner, "can I stay at Green Gables? Please tell me."

"Matthew and I would like you to stay," said Marilla, "but you must be a good girl. What's the matter, Anne?"

"I'm crying, but I'm not sad," said Anne. "I'm surprised and happy. No, happy is not the right word. I am more than happy!"

"You cry and laugh too easily," said Marilla.

"Can I call you Aunt Marilla?" asked Anne.

"No, you can call me Marilla. You will start school here in September," said Marilla.

"Marilla, will I have a best friend in Avonlea? I always wanted a best friend," said Anne.

"Diana Barry lives near here. She is eleven, too, and a very nice little girl. Maybe she will be your friend," answered Marilla.

"Does Diana have red hair, too?" asked Anne.

"She has black hair," said Marilla.

"That's good. I **hate** my red hair. But I like black hair. And, Marilla, I'm *very* happy to be Anne of Green Gables," said Anne.

"Good," said Marilla. "Now, go up to bed."

Two weeks later, Mrs. Lynde came to Green Gables. "I would like to meet your orphan," she said to Marilla. "I heard about the mistake at the orphanage. Why did you keep the girl?"

"We like her, Rachel," said Marilla.

Suddenly, Anne ran into the kitchen in her short yellow dress from the orphanage. She was surprised to see Mrs. Lynde.

"Well, she's not pretty, Marilla. She's too thin, and her hair is as red as carrots!" said Mrs. Lynde.

Anne was very angry. "I hate you!" she shouted at Mrs. Lynde. "You called me ugly and thin! You're a terrible person."

"Anne!" said Marilla, but Anne did not stop.

"You made me feel very bad. I will never **forgive** you!"

"Anne, go to your room," said Marilla.

Anne started crying and ran out of the kitchen.

"What a terrible child!" said Mrs. Lynde, angrily.

"You weren't kind about her hair, Rachel," said Marilla. "She was wrong to shout at you, but you were wrong, too."

Mrs. Lynde stood up quickly. "Well, I will not come here again! That little girl has problems. She is too angry. Good evening, Marilla!"

Mrs. Lynde left, and Marilla went to Anne's bedroom. Anne was on her bed. She could not stop crying.

"Anne, it was terrible to shout at Mrs. Lynde," said Marilla. "She wasn't kind about your hair, but you were too angry. You must go to Mrs. Lynde and say sorry."

"No! I can't do that. I'm not sorry," said Anne.

"You must, Anne. You'll stay in your room until you do," said Marilla.

Anne sat in her bedroom for two days. Marilla brought her food, but she did not eat anything. Matthew felt worried. At the end of the second day, he went to Anne's room.

"Please come out of your room and say sorry, Anne," said Matthew.

"Maybe I can do that for you," said Anne. "I *am* sorry now. I was very angry all night, but I'm not now."

"You're a good girl," said Matthew, and he left quickly.

Anne went down to the kitchen. "I'm sorry, Marilla," Anne said, quietly. "I was too angry. I'll say sorry to Mrs. Lynde."

"Very good," said Marilla. "Let's go to Mrs Lynde's house now."

They walked there together. Anne daydreamed and smiled a lot. "Why is she happy about this?" Marilla thought.

Mrs. Lynde opened the door, and Anne was at her feet. "Mrs. Lynde! I am *very* sorry. Please forgive me! I will *never* shout at you again. You only said *true* things to me—I am too thin, and I have hair as red as the reddest carrots!"

Mrs. Lynde was surprised. "Get up, child," she said. "I can see you are sorry. Now, go and play in the garden."

Anne went into the garden, and Mrs. Lynde turned to Marilla. "She is a strange girl, but maybe she is sweeter than I thought."

———————

"Did I say sorry well, Marilla?" asked Anne, on the walk home.

"Yes, Anne, but you said sorry a bit *too* well!" Marilla said with a little smile.

CHAPTER FIVE

Anne goes to church

"Well, do you like them?" said Marilla.

Anne looked at the three new dresses on her bed. "They're not very pretty," said Anne. "But I will try to like them."

"*Try* to like them!" said Marilla, angrily. "These are good, sensible dresses. I made them for you."

"I'm sorry, Marilla. That was very nice of you. But I would like a dress with puffed sleeves."

"Puffed sleeves are too expensive, and they look stupid," said Marilla. "Now, put your dresses away. You can wear one to **church** tomorrow." The next morning, Anne walked to Avonlea Church. Marilla could not go with her because she was sick.

Anne did not feel happy in her new dress. She also did not like her black hat. "How can I make it better?" she thought.

The answer came at the next corner. There were pink and yellow flowers near the road. Anne put lots of them on her hat, then ran happily toward Avonlea.

Lots of girls in pretty dresses were at the church. They were very surprised to see Anne in her flower hat! There were many strange stories about the orphan at Green Gables. They all looked at her but nobody talked to her.

Anne listened to the **minister** in the church. But he talked for a long time, and Anne started to feel very tired. She looked out the window at the trees and flowers until he finished.

———————

"How was church?" Marilla asked Anne at home.

"I didn't like it. It was terrible," answered Anne.

"Anne Shirley!" said Marilla, angrily.

"Well, I was a good girl. But I couldn't feel happy because every other girl there had puffed sleeves," said Anne.

"Don't think about your sleeves in church," said Marilla.

"The minister talked, but I didn't listen very much. He talked for too long," said Anne.

Marilla thought about Anne's words. The minister often talked for too long. Anne was a strange little thing, but maybe she was right.

CHAPTER SIX
Friends and enemies

Marilla did not hear about Anne's flower hat until the next Friday. "Anne, why did you do that?" she said. "Now everyone in Avonlea is talking about your strange pink-and-yellow hat!"

"It's true—pink and yellow don't look nice on me," Anne said.

"It's not the colors!" said Marilla, quickly. "Don't put flowers on your hat. It looks stupid."

"I'm sorry, Marilla. I thought they made my hat more beautiful." Anne started to cry.

"Don't cry," said Marilla. "Be more sensible next time. Now, I have some news for you. We are going to meet Diana Barry this afternoon."

"Oh, Marilla, that is wonderful! But will she like me?" asked Anne. She suddenly looked very worried.

"Diana will like you, but her mother is a difficult woman. Be a good girl, and don't talk too much. Then everything will be fine," said Marilla.

Mrs. Barry was a tall woman with black hair.

"Hello, Marilla, come in," she said. "Is this your orphan girl?"

"Yes, this is Anne," answered Marilla.

"Anne with an 'e'," said Anne.

Mrs. Barry showed Marilla and Anne into the house. Diana was on the sofa with a book. She was a pretty girl with a warm smile.

"This is Diana," said Mrs. Barry. "Would you girls like to play in the garden?"

The Barrys' sunny garden was a beautiful place. Anne could hear bees on the flowers, and a soft wind moved through the leaves in the trees.

"Diana," said Anne, quietly. "Will you be my *best* friend?"

Diana laughed. "OK. It will be nice to play together a lot. My sister cannot play with me. She is too young."

"Will you *always* be my best friend?" asked Anne, brightly.

Diana was surprised, but smiled kindly. "Yes, I would like that. I heard strange things about you, Anne, but I like you very much."

Later, Anne and Marilla walked home to Green Gables. "Well, are you and Diana best friends now?" asked Marilla.

"Yes! I am the happiest girl on Prince Edward Island," said Anne.

After a wonderful summer together, Diana and Anne started school in September.

Marilla was worried. "Will the other children at school like Anne? Will she talk too much?" she thought.

But Anne enjoyed school and made friends quickly. Every morning, Anne and Diana walked to school together.

"Look at this beautiful sunny day!" Anne said to Diana on their walk one morning. "I am happy to be on Earth today."

"It is very nice," said Diana. She did not like talking as much as Anne.

Avonlea School was a little white building near the road. There were pretty woods behind it and a small river.

"Look, Anne," Diana said. "There's Gilbert Blythe. He was away all summer."

Anne looked at Gilbert Blythe. He was a tall boy with brown hair and eyes, and a big smile. He pulled one of the other girls' hair.

"He isn't very kind," said Anne.

"He's funny! He's very intelligent, too. I like him," said Diana.

Gilbert sat at a desk near Anne in the lesson. He wanted Anne to look at him, but Anne looked out the window at the trees and flowers.

Suddenly, Gilbert pulled Anne's red hair and shouted, "Carrots! Carrots!"

Anne looked at him angrily. "You terrible boy! I hate you!"

She took her book and hit Gilbert on the head with it.

"Anne Shirley, what are you doing?" shouted the teacher, Mr. Phillips.

Anne did not
answer. She did
not want to
say "carrots."

"I was wrong,"
said Gilbert.
"I called her a
terrible name."

Mr. Phillips
did not listen.
"Anne, stand in
the corner for
the afternoon,"
he said. "You are too angry."

Anne did not cry, but she was very angry. "I will
never look at Gilbert Blythe again," she thought.
"I will never speak to him."

After school, Gilbert ran to Anne. "I'm sorry,"
he tried to say. But Anne walked past him quickly.
Now, Gilbert Blythe was her **enemy**.

CHAPTER SEVEN

A terrible mistake

It was a beautiful October morning at Green Gables. Anne watched the leaves on the trees turn yellow, orange, and red.

"I'm going to Carmody, the next village, this afternoon," said Marilla. "I won't be home before dark. Would Diana like to come over? You can have tea together."

"Yes!" said Anne. "Can we use the special cups?"

"No, but there is a bottle of raspberry juice in the cupboard. You and Diana can drink that," said Marilla.

Later, Diana came to the door in a pretty dress. "Please, come in," said Anne, nicely.

The girls sat down for tea and talked about school and their friends.

"I forgot the raspberry juice!" Anne said, suddenly. Anne found the bottle at the top of the cupboard. She put it on the table with a glass.

"Please have some, Diana," said Anne. "I'm not very thirsty."

Diana drank a glass of the raspberry juice. Then, Anne went to the kitchen, and Diana had a second glass.

"This is the best raspberry juice," said Diana, after Anne came back.

"Would you like more?" said Anne.

"Yes, please," said Diana. She drank a third glass.

Suddenly, Diana stood up very strangely and then sat down again.

"Diana, what's the matter?" asked Anne.

"I'm—I'm sick," she said, slowly. "I must go home."

"But you can't go home before the fruit cake. Lie on the sofa, and maybe you'll feel better," said Anne, worriedly.

"No, I must go now," said Diana.

Anne took Diana home, then cried on her walk back to Green Gables.

Two days later, Marilla sent Anne with a message for Mrs. Lynde. After a short time, Anne came back and ran to the sofa. She was crying very hard.

"What's the matter now, Anne?" said Marilla.

"Mrs. Lynde saw Mrs. Barry today. Mrs. Barry said I made Diana **drunk** on Saturday! Diana can't play with me again, she said."

Marilla looked surprised. "You made Diana drunk? What did you give her?"

"Only raspberry juice! Diana had three glasses of it."

Marilla looked in the cupboard and saw a half-empty bottle of wine. "Anne, you gave Diana wine! It wasn't raspberry juice."

"I didn't know! I didn't drink any," said Anne.

"The two bottles are the same color. You made a mistake, but it was easy to make. I will talk to Mrs. Barry and tell her about the mistake," said Marilla, kindly.

That evening, Marilla went to the Barrys' house, but she came back quickly.

"Is Mrs. Barry very angry with me?" asked Anne.

"Mrs. Barry is very difficult sometimes!" said Marilla. "She didn't listen to me. She won't forgive you. I'm sorry, Anne."

"I will never forget Diana," said Anne, sadly. She went to her room and wrote a letter.

My wonderful Diana,

You must listen to your mother and never see me again. But I will write every day, and we will always be friends.

Yours,
Anne (or Cordelia) Shirley

CHAPTER EIGHT

Doctor Anne

Anne and Diana did not play together for many months. Then, one January evening, Diana came to Green Gables. Her face was white, and she looked worried.

"What's the matter, Diana?" asked Anne.

"Anne, please come quickly!" Diana said. "My little sister, Minnie May, is sick, and my mother and father are away. She has a very bad **cough**—it's called croup. I'm very frightened."

Matthew stood up. "I will get the doctor from Carmody," he said.

"Don't cry, Diana. I helped lots of children with croup before I came to Green Gables. Let's go to your house," said Anne.

The two girls went into the cold winter night and ran through the dark woods.

Little Minnie May lay on the sofa at the Barrys' house. She looked hot and tired. Anne worked quickly. "Diana, I must have lots of hot water and medicine," she said.

Anne watched Minnie May all night and gave her medicine every hour. At 3 a.m., Matthew came with the doctor, but Minnie May's cough was better. She slept quietly on the sofa.

The doctor looked at Minnie May and smiled. "You did very well," he said to Anne. Matthew and Anne walked back to Green Gables. "Look, the sun is coming up," said Anne.

Anne went home and went to bed. She slept all day.

That evening, Marilla had news for Anne. "Mrs. Barry was here this afternoon," she said. "She wanted to thank you because you helped Minnie May. She wants you and Diana to be good friends again. Do you want to visit Diana tonight?"

Anne flew out of her chair. "Marilla!" she said. "This is very happy news. Can I go now? Can I wash the dishes later?"

"Yes, yes, go now," Marilla said, "but put on your hat first!" It was too late. Anne ran out into the snow and danced happily to the Barrys' house.

Queen's Academy

Anne and Diana played together for many more years on Prince Edward Island. One beautiful October, they got a new teacher—Miss Stacy.

"I like Miss Stacy more than any other teacher," Anne said to Marilla and Matthew. "She is intelligent and kind. And she always spells my name with an 'e'."

Anne was one of the best students in the class. Only one student was as good as Anne—her enemy, Gilbert Blythe. Gilbert tried to be friendly with Anne, but Anne could not forgive him.

One evening, Anne lay near the fire at Green Gables. Marilla looked at Anne in the warm light. She felt a great love for Anne.

"Miss Stacy was here today," said Marilla. "She is starting a special class for her best students, and she wants you in it. Some of the students in the special class will go to Queen's Academy one day. Queen's is a school for teachers. Would you like to study there and be a teacher, Anne?"

"Yes! But will it be expensive?" asked Anne.

"That doesn't matter. We'll pay. You're our child now," Marilla said.

Anne ran to Marilla and held her in her arms.

"Thank you, Marilla," Anne said.

———

Anne studied hard, but Gilbert Blythe worked hard, too. At the end of the school year, Anne and Gilbert were the two best students in Miss Stacy's class.

"You did it, Anne!" said Diana, on their last day at Avonlea School. "You got a place at Queen's Academy."

"I'm very happy," said Anne, "but I want you to come, too."

"Well, I'm not as intelligent as you. Maybe you and Gilbert will be friends at Queen's Academy," said Diana.

"Never!" said Anne.

———————

On a sunny September morning, Anne was ready to leave Green Gables.

"This is for you," Matthew said, and he held up a new dress. "I asked Mrs. Lynde to make it for you because you always wanted a dress with puffed sleeves."

"Matthew, it's beautiful!" said Anne, softly, with a big smile. "I will wear it today. Thank you."

Anne said a sad goodbye to Marilla and Diana. Then, Matthew drove her to Queen's Academy.

At Queen's, Anne and Gilbert were in the same class. Anne often looked at him across the classroom. "He's intelligent and works hard. Maybe I can be friends with Gilbert," she thought. "But we were enemies for too long."

The year there went very fast, and Anne and Gilbert were teachers at the end of it. Anne finished first in the class and got a place at Redmond College.

"I will study for four more years," Anne told Diana. "And Gilbert has a job—he will be the new teacher at Avonlea School from September."

Anne went back to Green Gables for the summer before college. "It's wonderful to be home," she said to Marilla on her first evening. "But, Marilla, is Matthew well?"

Matthew's hair was gray, and he looked sick.

"No, he isn't," said Marilla. "I'm worried about him. He must rest more."

"You look tired, too," said Anne.

Marilla smiled. "My eyes aren't good. I'm going to see a doctor about them."

Anne went into the garden and saw Matthew. He walked slowly toward the house. "You are working too hard, Matthew," she said. "Please will you rest more?"

"I can't, Anne. I'm old now, but I will work until I die," said Matthew.

"I want to be that boy from the orphanage now—I could help you more," said Anne.

"I need you more than a hundred boys. You're my girl," he said, smiling.

CHAPTER TEN
A different road

"Matthew—Matthew! What's the matter?" Marilla shouted. Anne ran in from the garden and saw Matthew on the kitchen floor. His face was very gray.

"Anne, go for the doctor," said Marilla, worriedly.

Anne came back quickly with the doctor, but it was too late.

Many people from Avonlea came to Green Gables. They said goodbye to quiet and kind Matthew Cuthbert. Anne brought flowers from the garden and put them near his body.

Later that summer, there was some more bad news.

"I saw the doctor today about my eyes. I am going **blind**," Marilla told Anne.

Anne could not speak.

"I must leave Green Gables, Anne. I can't do everything here as a blind woman. Someone will buy it," Marilla said, and then she cried very hard.

"You mustn't leave, Marilla! I will stay here. I won't go to college. I will be a teacher near Avonlea," said Anne.

"But college is very important to you," said Marilla.

"You are more important," said Anne.

A few days later, Mrs. Lynde sat with Marilla and Anne in the garden. "Well, Anne. I heard you're not going to college," she said.

"Yes, I will stay close to Marilla. I'm going to teach at Carmody School," said Anne.

"No, you're not. You'll teach here at Avonlea!" said Mrs. Lynde.

"But Gilbert Blythe has that job," said Anne.

"Gilbert heard your news and wanted you to have the Avonlea job. He's going to teach at a different school now. You must take the Avonlea job."

"I didn't know! Gilbert is very kind," said Anne.

The next evening, Anne saw Gilbert on the road to Avonlea. "Gilbert," she said with a red face, "thank you for giving me the Avonlea School job."

"I wanted to do something nice for you. Can we be friends now?" he said with a big smile.

"We were good enemies, and now we'll be good friends," said Anne.

Anne sat at her bedroom window for a long time that night. The wind blew softly in the cherry trees at Green Gables. "Everything is right in the world," she thought.

During-reading questions

CHAPTER ONE

1 Why does Mrs. Rachel Lynde sit at her window?
2 Where is Green Gables?
3 Why do Matthew and Marilla want an orphan boy?

CHAPTER TWO

1 Who is waiting at Bright River train station?
2 What does Matthew want Marilla to do at home?
3 What has the little girl always wanted?

CHAPTER THREE

1 Anne cannot stay at Green Gables. Why?
2 What does Anne think about a lot in her daydreams?
3 What happened to Anne's parents?

CHAPTER FOUR

1 What does Anne think about her red hair?
2 Mrs. Lynde says three terrible things about Anne. What are they?
3 What does Matthew ask Anne to do?

CHAPTER FIVE

1 Marilla makes three new dresses for Anne, but Anne does not like them. Why?
2 Marilla did not go to church with Anne. Why?
3 How does Anne make her hat better?

CHAPTER SIX

1 Why does Anne want Diana Barry to like her?
2 What does Gilbert Blythe do to Anne?
3 What does Anne do to Gilbert?

CHAPTER SEVEN

1 Why does Diana come to Green Gables for tea?
2 Marilla tells Anne, "You made a mistake, but it was easy to make." What happened?
3 Anne writes a letter to Diana. Why?

CHAPTER EIGHT

1 Why is Diana frightened?
2 Anne helps Minnie May. What does she do?
3 Marilla has news for Anne at the end of the chapter. What is it?

CHAPTER NINE

1 Why does Anne like her new teacher, Miss Stacy?
2 What does Matthew give Anne?
3 Why are Anne and Marilla worried about Matthew?

CHAPTER TEN

1 What happens to Matthew in this chapter?
2 Why must Marilla leave Green Gables?
3 Gilbert tells Anne, "I wanted to do something nice for you." What does he do?

After-reading questions

1 At the start of the book, Matthew wants Anne to stay but Marilla does not. Why?

2 Why is Anne's love of nature—trees, flowers, and animals—important in the story?

3 Why are puffed sleeves important to Anne?

4 At the end of the book, Anne thinks, "Everything is right in the world." Why does she think this, do you think?

5 How does Anne change in the story?

6 How does Marilla change in the story?

Exercises

CHAPTER ONE

1 Are these sentences *true* or *false*? Write the correct answers in your notebook.

1 Matthew Cuthbert is a loud man. ....*false*..........
2 Green Gables is near the other houses in Avonlea.
3 There are three plates on the kitchen table.
4 An orphan is coming from Nova Scotia.
5 Marilla wants to talk to Mrs. Lynde about the orphan.

2 **Write the opposite of the word in your notebook.**

1 quickly .... *slowly* ....   **2** beautiful
3 thin   **4** happy
5 late   **6** laugh

3 **Write the correct question word. Then, answer the questions in your notebook.**

1 .... *Who* .... is waiting for Matthew at the train station?
    A little girl.

2 .... does Matthew feel about meeting new people?
3 .... did Anne think about sleeping that night?
4 .... name does Anne want to be called?
5 .... is Anne too sad to do?
6 .... do Matthew and Marilla need a boy?

CHAPTERS THREE AND FOUR

4 **Complete these sentences in your notebook, using the words from the box.**

daydreamed	hate	mistakes	orphanage	sick

1 Anne looked out at the pretty garden and ..... *daydreamed* ..... for a long time.
2 "Where did you live before the ....?" asked Marilla.
3 Anne's mother got .... and died.
4 "I don't know much about children, and I will make ....," said Marilla.
5 "I .... my red hair," said Anne.

5 Match the two parts of the sentences in your notebook.

Example: 1—b

1 I would like a dress
2 Marilla could not go with her
3 Anne did not feel happy
4 There were many strange stories
5 Anne listened to the minister in

a because she was sick.
b with puffed sleeves.
c the church.
d in her new dress.
e about the orphan at Green Gables.

CHAPTERS SEVEN AND EIGHT

6 Write the past tense of these irregular verbs in your notebook.

1 Anne ......*found*...... (**find**) the bottle at the top of the cupboard.
2 Suddenly, Diana .... (**stand**) up very strangely and then sat down again.
3 Anne watched Minnie May all night and .... (**give**) her medicine every hour.
4 Minnie May .... (**sleep**) quietly on the sofa.
5 Anne .... (**fly**) out of her chair.

CHAPTER NINE

7 **Who said this? Write the answers in your notebook.**

Marilla

Matthew

Diana

1 "You're our child now." ....*Marilla*........
2 "Maybe you and Gilbert will be friends at Queen's Academy."
3 "This is for you."
4 "I'm worried about him. He must rest more."
5 "I need you more than a hundred boys."

CHAPTER TEN

8 **Order the words to make sentences in your notebook.**
1 quickly / came / too / with / it / the / Anne / doctor, /but /back /was / late.
  Anne came back quickly with the doctor, but it was too late.
2 I/ blind. / am / going
3 be /I/ Avonlea. / will / a / near / teacher
4 giving / Avonlea School / the / Thank / me / you / job. / for
5 We / now / be / friends. / were / and / good / we'll / good/ enemies,

61

Project work

1 The book is by Lucy Maud Montgomery. Look online. What things were the same for Lucy and Anne? Write a paragraph about it.

2 You are one of these people. Write a diary page.
  - Mrs. Lynde in Chapter Four.
  - Gilbert Blythe in Chapter Six.
  - Matthew in Chapter Nine.

3 Write a paragraph or a poem about something beautiful in nature.

4 In Chapter Seven, Anne writes a letter to Diana. Write a letter from Diana back to Anne.

5 Write a different end to the book. Anne goes to Redmond College. What happens to her and to Marilla?

An answer key for all questions and exercises can be found at **www.penguinreaders.co.uk**

Glossary

blind (adj.)
not able to see

church (n.)
A *church* is a building. People love God, and they meet in a *church*.

cough (n.)
You have a *cough* because you are not well. Air comes out of your mouth and makes a noise—often it happens again and again.

daydream (v. and n.)
You think about good things because you want them to happen, and you feel happy. "*Daydream*" is the noun of the verb "*to daydream*".

drunk (adj.)
not being normal because you had a strong drink. Wine (= a red or white drink made from fruit) can make you *drunk*.

enemy (n.)
Your *enemy* is not your friend. You do not like them, and they do not like you.

feel (v.)
past tense: **felt**
You can *feel* happy, sad, angry, or worried.

forgive (v.)
Someone does something bad to you, and you are angry. Then, after some time, you stop being angry with them. You *forgive* them.

hate (v.)
You *hate* a thing or person because you do not like them and sometimes you are angry with them.

minister (n.)
an important person in a *church*. People listen to what a *minister* says in *church*.

mistake (n.)
You do something wrong. You make a *mistake*.

orphan (n.); **orphanage** (n.)
An *orphan* has no mother or father. An *orphanage* is a home for *orphans*.

sensible (adj.)
(1) A *sensible* thing is right and good. (2) A *sensible* person does the right thing.

sick (adj.)
not well

suddenly (adv.)
Something happens quickly,
and you are *surprised*. It happens
suddenly.

surprised (adj.)
Something happens, and you did
not know about it before. You
are *surprised*.

terrible (adj.)
very bad

worried (adj.)
not happy, because maybe
something bad will happen